All The Strangers 1

A collection of poems

Emma Young

I

"Time was passing like a hand waving from a train
I wanted to be on. I hope you never have to think
about anything as much as I think about you."
Jonathan Safran Foer

Table of Contents

Table of Contents

For The Better

And so I repeat to myself
It's for the better
It's for the better
It's for the better

And I think about you while I wash
my hair and while I fall asleep at night
and while I eat dinner.

And I think about how it might be
for the better, but I never wanted better,
I just wanted you.

December

"If we make it through December" you
had said.

It's now another December and you
have been long gone.

The air is cold again and the love is still
there, for me, it's still there.

When I Breathe

And I feel it in my bones when I
breathe, this urge to call you and tell
you that I miss you.

Even though there is a chance you
won't say it back.

I Know I Will Leave This City

It's been a couple years now.

I'm sitting in a coffee shop when I hear your
laugh. I swear the cars stop honking and
everyone around me goes silent.

Like they can tell that my heart just stopped at
the sound of you.

I look at you, laughing with someone that is
not me.

For a minute, I just look at you, knowing you
don't see me. Maybe you haven't in awhile.

I look at your hair that I used to brush back
from your face and your eyes that used to
make me smile.

For a second, I'm tempted to go over to you,
and remind you of me, of what we had.

But I don't. I pack up my things and I walk out that door.

I keep walking, away from you, despite everything telling me to turn around.

Your laugh follows me down the street and so do my memories with you.

And I know that I will leave this city, with you in it.

Scared

I'm scared that I might never hear your voice calling my name again.

I'm scared that one day you'll move on and I'll be waiting for you to come back.

I'm scared that I might never get to hug you again and I won't remember the feeling of your arms.

I'm scared that our memories will continue to haunt me until the day I die.

I'm scared that I might have truly lost you this time and won't get you back.

I'm scared because you're who I want to love and I might never get to love you again.

Earth Calls Me In

It's been so long since I heard your voice.
Its been so long since we existed together.

But even after years have passed and people have come and
gone, I will remember you.

I will remember you when the birds chirp in the morning
and when the orange glow of the setting sun shines.

I will remember you when I am old and grey, until the
Earth calls me in.

Losing You Again

But at night, when everyone else was
asleep,

I was trying to stay awake so I didn't
have to see you in my dreams and lose
you all over again when I woke up.

Forever

But if you had just chosen me back, I
would have loved you forever.

Never mind that I already will love you
forever.

Drown

I would never beg someone to love me.

But the Earth drowned in my tears the
day that you left.

Begging

They say that love finds you when you
aren't looking for it.

But you found me when I was begging
on my hands and knees for someone to
love me.

And you left just the same.

With me begging on my hands and
knees for you to just love me.

Coldest of Days

I remember you on the coldest of days.

I met you in November and you left eventually when another year came around to March.

You are most familiar to me with your front facing the door.

One foot already stepping out, one foot inside, like I could maybe be worth fighting for.

Eventually you left, like most do.

But I foolishly begged maybe this time, the one who stayed would've been you.

Pieces

But she looked at you with such love, that if you shattered her heart over and over again, she would apologize for making a mess with the pieces.

Meet Me

Meet me at a place where the skies are blue and you still love me.

Meet me at a place where the grass grows and your hand is in mine.

Meet me at a place where the air smells like the ocean and we never said goodbye.

Meet me again at a place where we still exist.

Somewhere

Somewhere, there's a version of us that never said goodbye.

Somewhere, there's a version of us where loving each other was enough for the both of us.

Somewhere, there's a version of us that wasn't doomed from the start.

Somewhere, there's a version of us that said what we felt and not what we didn't mean.

Somewhere, there's a version of us where no one walked away.

Somewhere, there's a version of us that still exists.

I Still Had You

It'll be fall soon and I still love you as much as I did last fall.

Except last fall I still had you.

Better Than Anyone

You held my hand and said to me
"If the time was right, I'm sure we could have made it."

I looked at you with tears in my eyes and I said "I know."

I then walked away and I thought about how I could've
loved you better than anyone.

But we didn't make it, at least for now, and I know I'll be
thinking about it for the rest of my life .

Waiting For What?

There were thousands of handfuls of Earth
between us, but that didn't stop me from thinking
of you, hoping I'd see you again.

And I did see you again. On a hot humid evening
in mid July. You were sitting there nursing a cold
drink, waiting it seemed.

Waiting for what? I didn't know, but all I knew is
that you were never supposed to be this close. I've
learned to love you from a distance.

I didn't know what to do with seeing you in front
of me. I sat down next to you and you smiled, like
you knew I had been dreaming of you.

We talked about everything and nothing.

Evening turned to night and there wasn't another
place I wanted to be. I know you were only
visiting this town, but I was here to stay.

And I thought to beg of you, now that you are here, not to go. Now that I have held my love in front of you, do not leave.

I hadn't voiced these words, but by the way you were staring at me, I think you heard them.

Waiting for what? I didn't know, but I was always waiting for you.

Existence Among Mine

Sometimes I think about the emptiness of my bed
and imagine the weight of you next to me instead.
Your arm finding its way around me during the
night.

Or I think about cleaning the house and finding your
sock beneath the couch and your chapstick next to
the coffee machine.

I think about you and imagine my grocery list, in
between my handwriting is yours, where you
scribbled in last minute things.

I mostly think about just the closeness of you. Being
able to reach out for you and you are actually there.
Falling asleep next to you instead of falling asleep so
I can see you.

To have your existence among mine.

Shattered

The term "my heart shattered" sounds dramatic until the person that you love walks away and you are left picking up pieces of your heart in every place that reminds you of them.

Deathbed

And on my deathbed, I'll still remember you.

I'll remember your hands, the way you looked,
how you smelled, the way your eyes looked at
me.

And how my heart loved you more than it loved
anyone else.

Holding Heartbreak

I held my sister softly as her tears continued to fall. Most
of the words being whispered were
"but I loved him so much" as I replied "I know you
did."

How do you hold heartbreak and tell them the right
words? I will hold you so you don't break, but I can't say
anything to bring him back.

How do you hold heartbreak and tell them that you will
continue to see him everywhere but one day it won't hurt
as bad anymore?

I continued to hold heartbreak, that had taken the form
of my sister, and could only hope that she would see the
love in letting go.

Twenty

I liked to imagine, one day, running into you 20 years from now.

Maybe at a grocery store, we're both shopping for our families, the one we didn't end up having together.

Your eyes light up when you see me and the pain we caused each other is well in our past.

We catch up and laugh about all the heartbreak our young, foolish selves endured.

We say our goodbyes and return to our lives that moved on without the other.

And as I fall asleep that night, I remember you, 20 years ago, my hands in your hair, and my heart still in your hands.

Face

You were standing there with tears in your eyes, as we agreed that ending it was for the best.

And I stood there, taking in your features. Your eyes, your mouth, your hair, your dimples. And I swore to myself I would never forget your face.

It's been 8 years now and your features are starting to blur in my memories.

But sometimes, sometimes, you visit me in my dreams and your face is clearer than ever.

And I wake up from those dreams, with tears on my face, and I beg you to visit me again.

Hope

I hope you don't forget the way that I loved you.

I hope you don't forget the way that we laughed.

I hope you don't forget what we shared those summers.

I hope you don't forget the way that we looked at each other.

I hope you don't forget me.

Most importantly I hope I don't forget you.

Even If

I'll love you forever.

Even if you forget me and even if I don't want to.

Because isn't that what love is? Loving someone despite it all and for the hope of it all.

Curiosity

I dream of you being more curious, asking more questions. Of you meeting me halfway and not meeting me where it satisfies you best.

I dream of you holding me a little tighter and a little longer and kissing me softer. I dream of you placing your hands on my face and telling me that you could never love anything more.

But I wake up and you are never as curious, soft, or interested as I dream you to be. I wake up and I am met with the acknowledgment that just because I love you doesn't mean we work.

All The Strangers I've Ever Loved

All the strangers I've ever loved, are people I used to know more than I knew myself.

I loved you but now you are no longer mine to love.
I loved you but I don't know what your life is like anymore.
I loved you but we didn't survive.
I loved you but now you are a stranger.

For all the strangers I have ever loved.

Between The Lines

I write and I feel and I think about you too much.

And I'm trying to find you everywhere and I continue to find you nowhere.

So I pour my words out on paper and they all translate to "I miss you."

But your existence is far from mine and my words have come to replace us. I write and I write and you do not come.

And I realize somewhere between the lines of losing you and losing us, I lost myself.

This Feeling

I miss you. Can you feel it?
This feeling is too big for my body.
You have to be able to feel it too.

In My Sleep

I still know everything about you, and
yet we no longer talk.

How can the universe justify a stranger
walking around, who I could draw in
my sleep?

Some Days

Some days are better than others. If I
keep myself busy enough I can distract
my thoughts from wandering to you.

Other days my thoughts are persistent
and they demand to think of you. They
demand to miss you, and I just have to
let them.

I can go out as much as I want and
distract myself, but in the end, I know
I'm filling a void that was once your
voice.

I hope you know that I think of you. I
miss you with a desire that threatens to
make my heart explode. But I will try to
let you go.

Longing For You

I don't hate you and I never could.

But this longing for you is starting to
turn into something far from what it
used to be.

A plane I can't board.
A train I can't catch.
A race I can't win.

A love I can't have.

Silently Waiting

I was continuing on with my life but I
realized I was still silently waiting for
you.

In the background I was always hoping
you'd reach out again and tell me that
you missed me.

Reminiscing

I wonder, when you lay in bed at night,
do your thoughts drift off and do you
think about what we had?

Or am I alone in my reminiscing?

End

I felt the end of us before it ever
happened.

You were more distant, I was angrier.
You stopped listening, I stopped trying
to make you listen.

Our love had gone cold and I was
searching for ways to ignite the fire that
used to envelop our bodies.

But I knew it was time to go. I knew
that some love wasn't made to last, no
matter how much you loved them.

I felt the end of us, and the end of us
came.

A Little While

I know we weren't meant to last, but it
was nice to pretend that we were.

Just for a little while.

Think

And when I think about love, I think
about your face and your eyes.

And I think about all the time I spent
merging my existence with yours.

When I think about love, I also think
about pain and loss.

I think about saying goodbye and
watching your feet walk away.

I think about love and I think about
having and losing you.

Before and After

Time feels different when you say
goodbye to someone you love.

It becomes before them and after them.
Before love and after love.

Haunted

"Nothing else matters but you and me,"
you had once said.

You are gone now and our love is a
ghost, haunting me and reminding me.

I see you in places I go and people I
meet.

A shadow in the background chanting:
I'm here
I'm here
I'm here

But you aren't, your ghost is.

Thoughts of Me

It was cold, the air was dry, and the
wind was brisk.

That time of the year when people
don't pay much mind. Walking where
they have to go, a destination in mind,
not the journey. Eager to get warm.

Not you though, you liked the cold.
You said that the cooler air always
made you think clearer, sharper.

Now, when the air gets cold, I always
think about you. And I wonder what
you are thinking about. The thoughts
going through your head.

And I wonder if any of those thoughts
are of me.

Safe

I'll always keep my memories of you
safely tucked away. Safe from being
harmed.

Even if I don't always want to
remember them or think of them.

I like to just know that they are there.
So if maybe one day, I want to go back,
and just remember you and us, I can.

Know You

You have become someone I hear about
now, not someone I know.

I long to just know you like I used to.
I long to just hold you like I used to.

A Note From The Author

Thank you for coming along this journey with me and reading my first poetry book. I hope that you enjoyed reading it as much as I enjoyed writing it. Please feel free to follow along on my writing journey with me where it all started, on my TikTok page @lovercentral. Remember you are not alone.

Best, Emma

Made in the USA
Las Vegas, NV
04 February 2025

17457542R00031